Antarctica

Teaching Tips

Gold Level 9
This book focuses on developing reading independence, fluency, and comprehension.

Before Reading
- Ask readers what they think the book will be about based on the title. Have them support their answer.

Read the Book
- Encourage readers to read silently on their own.
- As readers encounter unfamiliar words, ask them to look for context clues to see if they can figure out what the words mean. Encourage them to locate boldfaced words in the glossary and ask questions to clarify the meaning of new vocabulary.
- Allow readers time to absorb the text and think about each chapter.
- Ask readers to write down any questions they have about the book's content.

After Reading
- Ask readers to summarize the book.
- Encourage them to point out anything they did not understand and ask questions.
- Ask readers to review the questions on page 23. Have them go back through the book to find answers. Have them write their answers on a separate sheet of paper.

© 2024 Booklife Publishing
This edition is published by arrangement with Booklife Publishing.

North American adaptations © 2024 Jump!
5357 Penn Avenue South
Minneapolis, MN 55419
www.jumplibrary.com

Decodables by Jump! are published by Jump! Library.
All rights reserved. No part of this book may be reproduced in any form without written permission from the publisher.

Library of Congress Cataloging-in-Publication Data is available at www.loc.gov or upon request from the publisher.

ISBN: 979-8-88524-790-0 (hardcover)
ISBN: 979-8-88524-791-7 (paperback)
ISBN: 979-8-88524-792-4 (ebook)

Photo Credits
Images are courtesy of Shutterstock.com. With thanks to Getty Images, Thinkstock Photo and iStockphoto. Cover – TerraceStudio, Kotomiti Okuma, Red monkey, Volodymyr Goinyk. p4–5 –NicoElNino. p6–7 -Harvepino, 2j architecture. p8–9 – VectorMine, Matt Makes Photos. p10–11 – Armin Rose, Fotos593. p12–13 – vladsilver Willyam Bradberry. p14–15 –Tory Kallman, reisegraf.ch. p16–17 – Ken Griffiths, Liam Quinn, Tarpan. p18–19 - U. Schzeibach. p20–21 – fivepointsix, demamiel62.

Table of Contents

Page 4   What Is a Continent?

Page 6   Antarctica

Page 8   Weather

Page 10   Living in Antarctica

Page 12   Animals

Page 16   Plants

Page 18   Exploring

Page 20   Sea Levels

Page 22   Index

Page 23   Questions

Page 24   Glossary

What Is a Continent?

A **continent** is a very large piece of land. There are seven continents on Earth. Six of the continents are split up into countries. Can you point to which continent you live on?

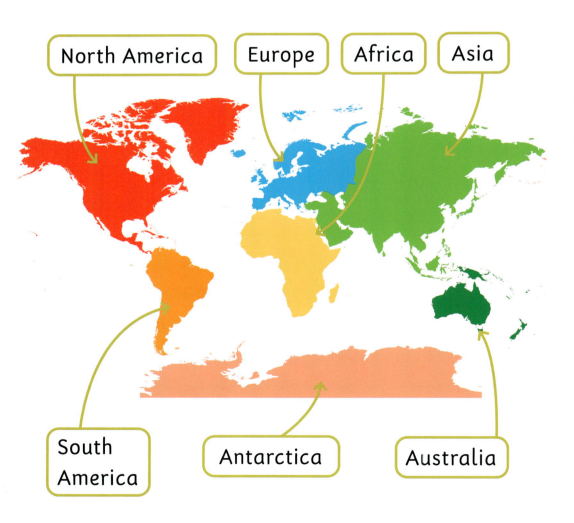

There are people living on each one of the seven continents. Asia is the continent with the most people living there. Each continent has different types of weather, landscapes, and ways of life.

Europe is a continent.

Antarctica

Do you know where Antarctica is? Antarctica is the continent that is farthest south. Antarctica does not have any countries. It is split into different parts called territories. Each territory is owned by different countries around the world.

Antarctica

Nobody lives in Antarctica forever. Scientists and workers live in research stations for a short time to learn about Antarctica. People sometimes visit Antarctica just to see what it is like there.

Research station in Antarctica

Weather

The **equator** is an imaginary line that runs around the middle of Earth. Places that are far away from the equator are usually colder than places that are close to it. Antarctica is one of the farthest places from the equator.

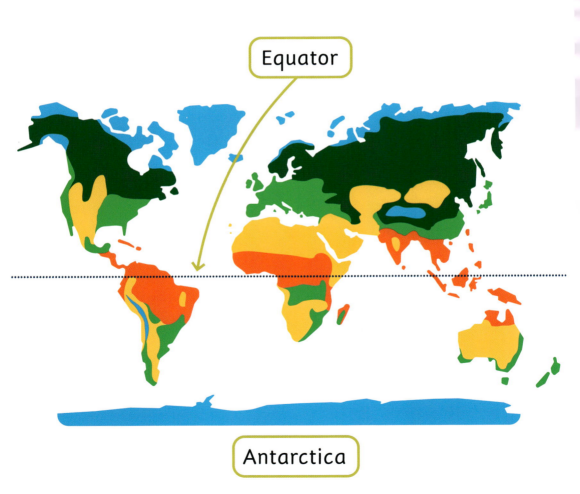

Antarctica is very cold, and there is a lot of wind. Most of Antarctica is covered in snow and ice all year. Some snow melts in the summer. Antarctica is called a **polar desert** because there is not much rain.

Living in Antarctica

The scientists who live in Antarctica study its weather, animals, plants, and rocks. They have to make sure they are dressed properly and keep warm. Around 3,700 people live in Antarctica in the summer.

It can be very hard to live in Antarctica. **Polar night** happens during winter. This is when there is usually no sunlight for around 30 days. The **southern lights** can be seen during polar night.

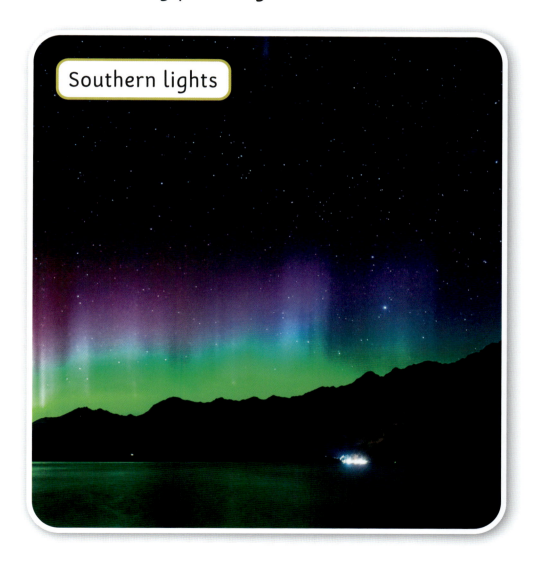

Southern lights

Animals

The animals that live in Antarctica have body parts that help them live in the cold weather. Emperor penguins have strong claws on their feet that help them walk on snow and ice.

Emperor penguins

Killer whales live in the waters around Antarctica. They have blubber under their skin that helps keep them warm. Killer whales are also sometimes called orcas. A group of killer whales is called a pod.

Killer whale pod

Albatrosses have very large wings. In fact, they have the longest set of wings of any bird on the planet! These large wings help them fly a long way to look for food.

Seals have large eyes that help them see underwater and catch other animals for food. Like killer whales, seals also have blubber under their skin that helps keep them warm.

Plants

Not a lot of plants can grow in Antarctica because of the weather. Plants that do grow there have special parts that help them survive. Antarctic hair grass has long roots that help it stay in place when it is windy.

Antarctic pearlwort grows near the coast where there is more water. Pearlwort flowers grow in summer.

On the islands around Antarctica, plant-like moss and lichen grow on rocks. A penguin might build a nest using moss.

Exploring

Lots of people have tried to explore Antarctica. The weather makes these trips very difficult. Many explorers have had to leave Antarctica early because of the weather.

Fabian Gottlieb von Bellingshausen was one of the first explorers to see land in the **Antarctic Circle**.

In 1911, Roald Amundsen became the first person to make it to the **South Pole**. The trip was very dangerous. It took two months for his group to reach the South Pole.

The place on Earth that is the farthest south is called the South Pole.

Sea Levels

Climate change is when the normal weather of a place changes over a long period of time. Antarctica is getting warmer because of climate change. This has caused some of the ice around Antarctica to start melting.

Melting ice and snow make the sea levels get higher. This can cause floods in other places around the world. Some animals could end up losing their homes because of climate change.

Index

animals 10, 12–15, 17, 21
climate change 20–21
continents 4–6
people 5, 7, 10, 18–19
weather 5, 8–10, 12, 16, 18, 20

How to Use an Index

An index helps us find information in a book. Each word has a set of page numbers. These page numbers are where you can find information about that word.

Page numbers

Example: balloons 5, 8–10, 19

Important word

This means page 8, page 10, and all the pages in between. Here, it means pages 8, 9, and 10.

Questions

1. Who was the first person to reach the South Pole?

2. Can you name a type of plant that grows in Antarctica?

3. What is something that happens during polar night?

4. Using the Table of Contents, can you find out which pages you can read about explorers on?

5. Using the Index, can you find a page in the book about people?

6. Using the Glossary, can you define what a continent is?

Glossary

Antarctic Circle:
An imaginary line that circles the Earth near the South Pole.

climate change:
Changes in Earth's weather and climate over time.

continent:
One of the seven large landmasses on Earth.

equator:
An imaginary line around the middle of Earth.

polar desert:
A region with cold temperatures and very little precipitation.

polar night:
When the Sun does not rise above the horizon.

southern lights:
Natural light displays in the sky.

South Pole:
The southernmost point of Earth.